GARETH O'CALLAGHAN

JOE'S WEDDING

Gareth O'Callaghan is one of Ireland's best-known radio presenters. He has been writing stories for over a decade, and lives in Dublin.

GEMMA

Open Door

JOE'S WEDDING
First published by GemmaMedia in 2009.

GemmaMedia
230 Commercial Street
Boston MA 02109 USA
617 938 9833
www.gemmamedia.com

Copyright © 2000, 2009 Gareth O'Callaghan

This edition of *Joe's Wedding* is published by arrangement with New
Island Books Ltd.

Printed in the United States of America
Cover design by Artmark

12   11   10   09   08   1   2   3   4   5

ISBN: 978-1-934848-10-4

Library of Congress Preassigned Control Number (PCN) applied for

OPEN DOOR SERIES

Patricia Scanlan
Series Editor

OPEN DOOR

CHAPTER ONE

Today is the day I get married.

It was the only message that flashed across Joe Mooney's mind as he opened his eyes. The deep blue sky and the bright sun blinded him. The fresh westerly wind made his teeth chatter. The coldness and force of the wind against his face seemed strange. It's a dream, he kept telling himself. You're nervous so you're dreaming.

Someone must have left his bedroom window wide open all night. The sunlight was everywhere. There was nothing covering him. There were no blankets at his feet. He tried to open his eyes again. The insides of his eyelids felt rough and gritty. Where the hell had the roof gone? *"I'm freezing!"* he roared. He popped his head up to check the bedside clock. He reached over to close the window. There was no clock. There was no window. All Joe could see was miles and miles of blue sky. He felt below him. Grass. Lots of it. Long grass and weeds.

It dawned on him that he wasn't in his own bed. His eyes stung. His head throbbed and his neck hurt. His brain didn't want to obey the order to think. He raised his head to survey his location.

Then he looked down towards his feet. *"Sweet Jesus!"* he screamed.

His clothes shocked him wide awake. He was wearing red nylon tights, shiny black plastic shoes, and a blue polo neck with a huge crest on the front and a yellow cape.

Panic set in. He sat up and looked around. He had been sleeping on a park bench. It was cold and damp. He could see blue, choppy water. In front of him was a lake. He squinted and made out two small fishing boats. "That's not a lake," he said to himself. "I've never seen fishing boats on a lake." He watched them, bobbing about in a rough sea. What sea?

"Where am I?" he asked. He looked around slowly in an effort to get his bearings. Surely there was a shop he would recognise, he thought, or a car, or a hotel since this was a seafront. No cars. No hotels. No shops. He was sitting on a rusty park bench, dressed as Superman.

Worse again, he was lost.

He checked for money. There were

no pockets in the tights, which were almost ripped to shreds by now. Where did I put these clothes on? Who gave them to me? What did I do while I was wearing this outfit? he wondered. The last question made him feel sick. The night before started off as an unofficial "few drinks" with his mates. He refused to call it a stag, because stags always got out of hand.

"No tying me up to lampposts, you hear me?" he'd warned the lads. "No polish, I'm warning you." He checked his outfit again. He would have opted for the polish any day, compared to this. "Wait till I get you. Just wait until your big days come around," he said angrily, trying to imagine the fun they all must have had. He tried to remember. He quickly gave up. From about ten the night before until ten minutes ago, he could recall nothing. It just didn't exist.

He searched under the bench. "What did I do with my money?" he shouted. Don't panic, Joe! he told himself. There's got to be a perfectly good reason why you're sitting here on a park bench. He waited, expecting an answer. He closed his eyes and cursed.

CHAPTER TWO

It was all slowly coming back to him now. The pub crawl, the Tequila slammers, the kissogram girl … the boat. "Oh Jesus, Mary and Joseph!" he whispered. Five of his mates had bought him a present and asked Linda, the kissogram, to present it to him. It was a ticket to Holyhead. He quickly searched himself. "There must be a return voucher," he muttered, running his hands through his cape and down the insides of his red tights. There was nothing. Nothing.

He sat back on the bench and took three deep breaths. He had no watch so he had no idea what time it was. For all he knew it could well be three o'clock, the time he was due to marry Liz Gunner in the Church of Our Lady of Sorrows.

He thought about the word "sorrows" for a moment. It had become his nickname for Liz: Mother of Sorrows. She was such a serious person. Everything had to be a crisis. Even when Joe brought her out for a drink with the lads, she would end up giving them all advice. Joe used to say, "Liz, will you shut up, *please*! Or I'll lose all my friends."

He tried to remember to whom he had been chatting. Had he made a show of himself in front of anybody? To hell with them, he thought. If they didn't like the party they should have gone home. Joe Mooney was boss. He was his own man, free to do whatever he wanted, and to hell with the begrudgers.

His mind was totally confused, apart from the brain damage caused by gallons of beer, washed down with countless slammers. He lay back down on the seat and willed himself to die. *"Oh God, please don't do this to me. Please, help meee!"* he kept crying out until he felt his voice going hoarse. He lay still for a while and worked on a number of solutions. One: he could go back to the ferry ticket office and pretend he had been booked to entertain the passengers on the return crossing. Two: he could ring the local television station and tell them he had been dragged into a car the night before. He was leaving a pub in Dublin at the time. His kidnappers dropped him off in Holyhead after robbing him of everything. Or three: he could phone Liz and tell her the truth. With a bit of luck she might call off the wedding.

Joe knew there would be no such luck.

There was only one problem: he had no money to make the phone call. He lay there, staring up at the blue sky. He was getting dizzy again. Three seagulls flew in circles above his head.

"Excuse me, are you Superman?" a slow deep voice asked.

Joe Mooney sat up and looked behind him. An elderly man wearing waders stood looking at him. He wore a tatty jacket tied at the waist with baling twine and a black cap. He was standing directly behind Joe now, blocking out the sun.

"No, I'm not Superman," Joe said

anxiously. "Can you tell me what time it is?"

The old man shook his arm. He waited for his watch to slide down to his wrist. "It's twenty-past nine. That's my bench you're sitting on."

Joe moved to one end of the bench. "Since when did you own this bench?"

"I've sat down here every single day for as far back as I can remember, son; sometimes twice a day. How many times have you sat down here?"

"Never. This is my first and last time."

"Well then, since it's my bench I don't mind sharing with you."

CHAPTER THREE

The old man sat down beside Joe and extended his hand. "My name is Marty. Pleased to meet you …"

Joe half-looked sideways. The old man's face was full of deep lines. It was well-tanned and healthy looking. He looked tired but relaxed. "Joe's the name." He wasn't going to shake hands with the beggar who'd been up to his elbows in every bin in wherever he was. "Now will you do me a favour and push off? I'm trying to sort out a little problem here."

"Well, Joe, I always say to people, a problem halved is a problem shared. Maybe I can help you work it out. I can give you a few minutes."

Joe looked at Marty. "*Get lost, will you!*" he shouted.

Marty bowed his head slightly. "There's no need to be so bad-tempered, young fella. It's been a long time since anybody spoke to old Marty like that. Is something bothering you?"

"Yes. I'm supposed to be getting married today."

"That's *wonderful*. I'm so happy for you. You must be over the moon with excitement. Mind you, you sound like someone who's going to a funeral, not a wedding." Marty made himself comfortable. "I remember when I got married." He rubbed his chin and fixed his hat on his head. "It was the happiest day of my life, quite some time ago I have to admit. My God, when I think back, she looked beautiful, did my Cathy. What time is the wedding?" Marty asked.

"Three. But I don't think I'm going to make it. Maybe that's not such a bad thing."

"Why not, Joe?"

Joe slapped his knees and kicked the seat. "Slight problem. I'm meant to be getting married in Dublin."

"*Dublin!* And what are you doing here?"

"It's a long story. Do you mind me asking you where exactly we are?"

Marty was amused by Joe's question. "Holyhead. You're in north Wales, lad! You're overlooking the Irish Sea, Joe. Isn't it gorgeous?" Marty admired the view. "One of the most beautiful mornings we've had all year. We don't usually get this sort of fine weather in November. I guess God was in one of his better moods when he woke up this morning. It's been raining non-stop for the past two weeks here. You'd have caught your death lying there if it had been last night." Marty smiled. "Anyway, how come you're here in Holyhead on the morning of your wedding?"

"A few of my friends decided to play a cruel joke on me when I was drunk last night. They got me into a taxi and drove me down to the car ferry and put me on it."

Marty looked confused. "What's so funny about that?"

"Nothing, I guess. Probably just trying to get me back for all the cruel jokes I played on them down through the years."

"Have you called home?"

"I don't have any money."

"Well, are you going to go back on the boat?"

"I don't have a ticket."

"Sounds pretty nasty, Joe. You're kind of stuck in limbo. Not looking too good for your wedding."

Joe sighed. "Guess so."

"How come you're dressed up as Superman?" Marty asked.

Joe looked down at the clobber. "I haven't a clue. Look, what do you want anyway? You're making my headache worse with your stupid questions. I don't have any money, OK? I'd give you some if I had it. So why don't you just piss off and let me work this out."

Marty stared at Joe before turning and gazing at the sea. "You don't really mean that, do you, Joe? I reckon if I stood up now and walked away you'd be off that bench like a scared cat running after me."

"Please … just go away. Do your begging somewhere else. I'm not interested."

"What did you just say there, Joe … *begging*? Do you really think I'm a beggar? I'm not a beggar. And if I wanted your money I'd have robbed you blind hours ago while you were in a drunken coma on this bench. Just because I dress like this doesn't mean I'm poor. Nor does it mean I'm weak. I was a champion boxer in my day. I've got medals and trophies to prove it." Marty clenched his fist. "You see that?" He held it under Joe's chin. "That could take your head clean off with one hard left-hook."

"Yeah, right," Joe mocked. "You've been drinking too much cheap wine, old man."

"No. I don't drink, Joe. I like to keep a clear head. I never know who I'm going to meet. My clothes might look a bit odd. But that's all. You can't judge someone's heart by the clothes they wear, or the face they have. It's just like you. You're dressed up as Superman, the action hero – every kid's favourite. But there's nothing *super* about you, Joe. You're just a rude, arrogant kid."

"I'm not a kid! And I'm not rude and arrogant."

"Really? I'd hate to see you on a bad day," Marty said quickly. "How old are you?"

"Twenty-five."

"Well, start behaving like a twenty-five-year-old instead of some jumped-up little kid who's just turned thirteen. What do you work at?"

"I sell cars."

"Do you like your job?"

"Yes."

"Do you sell many cars?"

Joe thought for a moment. "Enough to get me by."

"How many decent cars do you sell, Joe?"

"All the cars I sell are decent."

"How many lies does it take to sell one of your cars?"

"I'm not a liar."

"You're not talking to a customer now, Joe. I'm not standing on your forecourt putting all my trust in what you're telling me, and handing over all the hard-earned cash it's taken me years to make. Have you ever sold a dodgy car, Joe?"

"I don't know what you mean."

Marty laughed heartily. "Of course you do, Joe. Picture this: you're trying to flog a five-year-old car that's got a suspect history. You bought it from a scrap dealer who bought it from a guy who'd crashed it badly. Now you know

I know nothing about cars. I trust your every word beyond a shadow of a doubt. If I was to ask you has this car been involved in a crash, would you tell me the truth?"

Joe roared laughing. "Of course not! What do you take me for … a complete fool? If I tell you that car had been wrapped around a lamppost, would you buy it?"

"Of course not. But I'd be surprised that you were trying to sell it to me in the first place. I'd warn everyone not to go near you."

"That's why I wouldn't tell you in the first place. Looks are deceiving, Marty. The same goes for cars also."

Marty smiled. "I guessed you'd say that. Now picture this: if Liz, your wife, fell in love with that same car in your showroom and told you she had to have it, would you let her drive it?"

"Of course not!" Joe said instantly.

"Well, what's the difference?" Marty asked.

Joe mulled over his question. "What do you mean, what's the difference? The difference is that a customer who walks in off the street is a stranger who I'll probably never see again, so I don't have to worry that I sold him a dodgy car, and the other is my future wife, you idiot!" Joe raised his finger. "Hang on a minute, how did you know her name is Liz?"

"Because you told me a few minutes ago."

"Did I?" Joe said.

CHAPTER FOUR

"What time is it?" Joe asked anxiously, standing on the bench to see what was over the wall behind him.

"It's a quarter to ten. Relax, Joe. You've nearly three hours to get to the church. Why don't you wear the Superman outfit instead of a tuxedo?"

"Because I'd look a right fool, that's why."

"But you are a right fool, Joe."

"How dare you! I don't need to listen to you. I've got enough to worry about without listening to your nonsense." Joe sat down again. "I don't suppose you'd have a spare cigarette on you?"

Marty smiled. "You know, you said that like you'd expect me to say it. Isn't that right?"

"I don't understand."

"You still think I'm a beggar. You still expect me to bum a few quid off you, ask you for a cigarette. Isn't that right, Joe?"

Joe ignored him.

"Sorry, I don't smoke. Tell me all about this beautiful girl you're marrying today."

Joe frowned. "She's not beautiful. She's fat and she's ugly, and I don't know why I'm getting married to her."

"You know something, if she had been within hearing distance when you said that, I'd have slapped you around the place. How dare you call this woman fat and ugly!"

"How the hell do you know what she looks like?" Joe shouted angrily.

"I don't know. All I know is that no one grew up with the intention of being fat and ugly." Marty leaned closer to Joe. "Let me have a good look at you for a minute." He sat back. "You're no oil painting yourself, Joe. I think you look just average. I'm sure Liz's friends have asked her what the hell she sees in you."

"No they haven't."

"I bet they've said, 'Liz, why don't you try and find someone more handsome … someone with a bit of style and class … someone who really likes you for who you are?'"

"Rubbish."

"Do you love her?" asked Marty.

"No. Most definitely, *no*!"

"They why are you marrying her?"

"I don't know. I suppose because it's

the done thing. Even though we've been together less than a year, she kept hinting at it. And it seemed like a good idea at the time …" Joe trailed off.

"So why don't you call it off? Do yourselves a favour."

"Are you for real? Her parents would kill me. Her father would go and get his shotgun and finish off whatever's left of me."

"So who are you doing this for, Joe?"

"Jesus Christ, Marty, no wonder you're on your own. Is this the way you always behave around friends?"

"Who said we're friends, Joe?"

CHAPTER FIVE

Joe stared at Marty. He knew there was more to this sweet old man than met the eye. His questions were making him very nervous. I never mentioned Liz, he said to himself, watching the old codger as he stared longingly out to sea. I definitely never mentioned her name. How did he know?

Marty pointed to the sea. "I used to be a fisherman. I know those waters like the back of my hand. I often spent weeks out there dropping nets, pulling full catches in over the side of the deck. There was no refrigeration in those days. We used salt water to keep the fish from rotting." He looked at Joe. "I love the sea. There's something scary and magical at the same time about its power. And yet there's something beautiful about how it can just turn about face and become as tranquil as a millpond. Do you like the sea, Joe?"

Joe sniggered. "No, it makes me puke."

"You only know how much you love things when you get old, Joe."

"What are you talking about now, Marty?" It was a loaded question.

"Our women. Our partners. It took me years to realise how important my Cathy was to me She's still my soul mate, I suppose … everything I ever wanted. And you know something, I never realised that until a few years ago."

"Yeah, well you're welcome to Liz. I

wish someone would take her off my hands. She never shuts up talking about stupid things."

"They're not stupid to her. What sort of things?"

"She never gives up talking about the house. What she's going to do with this room, and how she's going to paint the kitchen yellow. And paper the hall, stairs and landing with Laura Ashley. Jesus, I can't stand it when she starts that stuff. I just have to get out."

"And what do you talk about to her? The silver Audi you conned someone into buying that afternoon?"

"I don't bother talking to her. There's no time left anyway once she's finished talking to me. She babbles on for hours about nothing."

"Have you ever thought that maybe she loves chatting with you, Joe? Maybe you're the first decent human being she gets a chance to talk to all day."

"I can't stand being near her."

Marty sighed. "That's not good."

"I'm just thinking wouldn't it be great if, when I got home, she'd been killed in a car accident. That would solve all my problems."

"You don't mean that, Joe. That's a shocking thing to say about anybody, whether you like them or not. It's really awful to hear you saying it about the woman you are about to marry."

"Jesus, do you have to keep reminding me?"

"You said something interesting just there, Joe. 'That would solve all my problems,' you said. What did you mean by that?"

"Liz is a compulsive spender. I seriously believe she has some sort of problem."

"What does that mean?"

"It means she spends all of my money."

"Well, your money is her money. Does she not have money of her own?"

"Of course she has money of her own. But the money she earns at work wouldn't stretch from Thursday to Saturday, so she takes mine."

"Takes it or asks for it?"

"Well, she'd ask me for fifty quid."

"That's not a lot. What would she do with the fifty quid?"

"*Spend it, of course!*"

"On what?"

"What is this – twenty questions? She'd spend it on supermarket stuff."

"Ah! So she's thinking of you as she's spending it. 'Let me see now, what would Joe like for his dinner tomorrow evening? Mmm, chicken stuffed with cheese and chive sauce, rolled in bacon. Very nice. Oops, it's a wee bit expensive but – what the hell – my Joe is worth every penny of it. And I know he loves stuffed chicken.' Is that what she's thinking, Joe … of you?"

"Maybe."

"She sounds like a lovely girl. What does she work at?"

"She's a checkout assistant in the local supermarket."

"You make it sound like she's not important. Does she like her job?"

"I don't know. I never asked her."

"You don't need to ask her. Maybe she's been telling you for years how much she hates it. On the other hand, maybe she loves it. Some of us enjoy meeting different people throughout the day. My Cathy used to work in a little corner shop. She'd have lots of customers day and night. You know why? Because all those people were looking for a friendly face. Someone who would just chat to them and listen to what they had to say for a few minutes each day. More importantly, someone who would just listen to their problems. All my Cathy had to do was ask, 'How are you?' She would end up standing there for ten minutes listening to the answer to that simple question. And you know, Joe, that little old woman would leave that shop with a spring in her step. She'd shared her story with a friendly face. She'd got a whole load of worries off her mind. Worries that maybe her husband wasn't interested in listening to because he was too wrapped up in himself. And my Cathy's tiny little corner shop was ten times more popular than the local supermarket."

"I don't need to sit here listening to

this rubbish. I've got to find a way of getting back on that boat and getting home in time for the wedding. She'll kill me if I'm late."

Marty smiled. "You won't be late, Joe. I'll see to that."

"Just how are you going to do that?"

"Leave it to me, I'll have a word in the right ear. I'll have you back on the 11.30 a.m. sailing to Dublin, I promise. It's only ten; we've plenty of time."

"How the hell do you know what time it is? Are you some sort of mind reader or something?"

"No, I looked at my watch a minute ago." Marty started to laugh. "Don't tell me I'm scaring you, Joe."

Joe sniggered. "You don't scare me, old man. You just sit there and talk to yourself, and let me figure out a way of getting home, OK?"

"OK, Joe. While you're figuring out

a way of getting home, I hope you don't mind me chatting. Do you?"

"Fire away. Ask me what you want. But just let me ask you one question first."

"OK."

"Who are you and what do you want from me?"

"That's two questions. Two very valid questions, I have to admit. I'm Marty, plain old Marty. I love to just sit here every morning. I love thinking back over all the memories of what's been a wonderful life. It's a nice way to live, Joe. As for the second part of your question, what do I want from you? Absolutely nothing, Joe. I just want to share a little bit of your time and goodwill. It costs nothing, just a few minutes. And from where I'm sitting, you've got a bit of time on your hands this morning.

Isn't this a nice way to spend a morning, Joe?"

"No it's not. It's sad. I could be doing worthwhile things, like selling a couple of cars to pay for this bloody wedding reception. You know how much this scam is costing me? Eight and a half thousand pounds. Jesus, I must be mad in the head. I could be back in Dublin making three times that much money for the time I'm wasting here talking to you. There's plenty of money to be made out there. I intend being rich by the time I'm thirty … retired by thirty-five and living on my luxury yacht in Marbella. None of that 'thinking of the old days' nonsense for me."

"What's more important to you, Joe? Your yacht or your lovely wife?" Marty sat back on the bench, watching Joe decide.

"My yacht."

"But you don't have a yacht yet."

"But I will have a yacht."

"Says who? I don't see any flash businessmen around here. All I can see is a grumpy, angry kid dressed up as Superman. I wouldn't buy a car from you if I knew you wandered around park benches dressed up as a superhero, Joe."

Joe watched Marty, his eyes opening wide. "Who are you? Some sort of undercover policeman?"

It was Marty's turn to laugh warmly. "No, I'm not a cop. I'm not a beggar either. I'm just a retired fisherman who hung up his nets a long time ago."

CHAPTER SIX

Joe became distracted by the sound of rustling. He looked across at Marty who had his hand deep in his pocket, fiddling with something. Joe watched as Marty pulled a large paper bag through the small opening. He placed the package on his lap and opened it with great care.

"What's that?" Joe asked.

"Cheese and pickle sandwiches. Real brown bread. Good and healthy. There's enough for the two of us. Would you like one?" Marty held up the brown wholegrain sandwich. The cheese had gone hard and turned brown.

"No thanks," Joe said, feeling queasy at the prospect. "Where did you get them? In a bin somewhere?"

Marty paused from biting into the sandwich and stared at Joe. "I beg your pardon, kid. I am not a beggar – well, certainly not in the sense that you understand. I got these sandwiches on the boat."

"What *boat*?" Joe asked.

Marty munched contentedly. "On the same boat you were on."

"So you saw me?"

"Couldn't miss you. You made a right show of yourself on that crossing last night. Do you remember trying to fly off the bar counter? You landed on a bunch of German tourists … spilt all their drinks. Oh, you were the real funny man all right. Then you got all nasty and hateful when they asked you to buy them another round. You started to imitate Hitler, telling them they were responsible for mass murder. The barman called the purser. He gave you a stern warning. My God, Joe, what kind of man are you?"

"It was only a bit of fun. Anyway those Germans have no sense of humour."

"I'd be inclined to disagree with you, Joe. My Cathy was German, and she was one of the funniest people I have ever met in my entire life. I sometimes think that's one of the secrets of a long and happy marriage: being able to laugh together … being able to laugh at each other. I know a doctor who used to tell his patients to laugh a bit more. He'd get them to stand up in his surgery. *'Laugh!'* he would shout at them. *'Harder!'* 'Once you can laugh,' he used to say, 'you're well on your way to recovery.'

"What a load of twaddle." Joe practically spat out the words.

"I'd say you could do with bottling a little of your wife-to-be's laughter, Joe."

"How do you know Liz laughs?"

"I just guess that she needs to be able to laugh a lot to marry someone like you. She must have a great sense of humour. She must have a lovely laugh."

"Are you being smart?"

"Yes, Joe, I am smart. Many people down through the years have told me, 'Marty, you're a pretty smart guy.' I guess I am. Do you know why I think that woman of yours has a sense of humour? Because if she didn't she wouldn't be marrying you. Do you want to know why?"

"Why?"

"I'll tell you why, Joe: because you are a self-righteous, mean and nasty, barky old fart. If you were my age, I'd just put it down to regret on your part. Sadness that you didn't realise sooner that *you* – not anyone else, just you – were responsible for destroying your own happiness and peace of mind. Regret that you let all the chances you were given to see how wonderful this short life really is pass you by. You know what I can't get over, Joe? The fact that you're only twenty-five. You're only a child, but a very dangerous child, it must be said."

"*Shut up!*" Joe shouted.

"See what I mean … lashing out like a two-year-old."

"Why am I *dangerous*?" Joe asked.

"I'll tell you why you're dangerous, Joe. You're at an age and a stage in your life when you could easily destroy the lives of a lot of people close to you."

"Like who?"

"Like the man who bought that Jeep from you yesterday afternoon. You didn't give him the attention he deserved. You almost ignored him, yet you took a cheque for a lot of money from him. Far more than that heap of junk you sold him is worth."

Joe looked stunned. "How did you know I sold a Jeep yesterday?"

"Because on the boat last night I got chatting with the bloke who bought it. He's taking his family to Disneyland, in Paris. He's travelling with his wife. They have three small children and a ten-month-old baby. You never told him that that Jeep had been in a crash. It was written off three months ago. You never told him that you'd bought it from a crooked insurance broker who had carried out the assessment on it for the original owner, did you, Joe?"

Joe looked baffled, weary from the beating he was taking. "How do you know all this?"

Marty tapped the side of his nose. "There are ways of finding out, Joe. It's not that difficult. And I've got news for you. He's not going to Disneyland. He's down there at the pier, waiting to load that heap of junk that you sold him back onto the boat for Dublin. He's going to be calling on you to get his money back."

"Did you tell him everything you knew?"

"Let's just say I planted a seed of doubt in his mind. He told me he didn't feel comfortable driving it. Can you blame me for telling him? Did you really think that Jeep was going to make it through a twelve-hundred-mile round trip to Paris?"

"Jesus Christ, why can't you just mind your own business? This could destroy my business, do you know that?" Joe argued.

"You're already on the verge of bankruptcy, Joe. You don't need to lose money to go bankrupt. I'd say – no matter how much money you make selling dodgy cars between now and the time you're thirty-five – you'll always be bankrupt."

"I don't sell *dodgy* cars." Joe dropped his voice. "Well … maybe the odd car slips through that doesn't get my full attention."

"Bullshit!" Marty snapped.

Joe's eyes opened wide. He was surprised by the old man's bad language.

"Picture this: he's driving along the

motorway in France in the Jeep you sold him … slowly pushing it up through the gears. Sixty. Seventy. Seventy-five. His eight-year-old daughter is urging him from the back seat to drive faster. His wife is minding their baby, giving her breakfast. The other daughters are playing 'I Spy With My Little Eye'. Unfortunately the driver hadn't spotted the signs. The bearings in the front left wheel are all damaged because the chassis is bent, Joe. The wheel comes loose and flies up on to the bonnet of a car travelling in the opposite direction. It goes through its windscreen like a tomahawk missile. Within seconds everyone in that car is dead. Meanwhile, the man in the Jeep suddenly realises that he's missing a front wheel. The Jeep dips to the left. Now there's no steering. The Jeep has taken on a mind of its own. It slams into the steel fencing that runs down the centre of the motorway. Then it somersaults and eventually lands on its roof a quarter of a mile down the road. Just as the man you sold the Jeep to is trying to remember your name, the Jeep explodes into flames."

Marty took a long, deep breath and sighed. "I guess when you read about it in the Irish papers the next day, you'd probably just chalk it down to experience. I guess you'd be getting down on your knees and giving thanks that no one is ever going to point the finger at you, Joe."

Joe was silent, staring out at the choppy breakers that looked so small from where they were sitting.

"But you don't have to worry, Joe. It's not going to happen. He'll be calling to you tomorrow to get his money back.

"It's OK, Joe. I gave him the name of the hotel where you'll both be staying. He said he'd call by in the morning. Not too early, I told him. Just make sure you have his money for him when he calls."

"*Fourteen thousand pounds?* Where the hell am I going to get that sort of money between now and tomorrow morning?" Joe stood up and started to walk in circles in a panicky sort of way, shouting and muttering.

CHAPTER SEVEN

"Who is the most important person in your life right at this moment, Joe?" Marty sat back and stared out at the fishing boats closing in on the harbour.

"Me," Joe replied. "Are you surprised by that?"

Marty shook his head. "Joe, that's why your life is always so complicated. You're losing the message here. It's staring you in the face."

"What are you talking about?" Joe asked brazenly.

"If you don't think about yourself so much, leave a bit of time for other people, life becomes a real joy. You begin to see things, things you never knew existed."

"Like what?"

"Like other people's love for you. Like the happiness you bring them which they return."

Joe threw his hands up in the air. "You've lost me."

"Let me explain something to you. I have a son who's a few years older than you. You might as well be him, Joe. You're cheeky and you're stubborn. You won't take advice. All my life I tried to fill that boy's head with some decent attitude. All I got for it was abuse. He called me every name under the sun. I should have thrown him out of the house, but I couldn't because I loved him. He was my own flesh and blood. I kept asking God to change him. I kept hoping I would wake up some morning and he would be different. He was the coldest, most hurtful person I knew. I kept blaming myself for the way he turned out. I told myself I must have done something wrong when he was a young kid and this was the result. I felt I was responsible for his cruel, greedy, narrow outlook on life. It took something awful for that to change."

Marty stopped talking. He leaned forward and buried his face in his hands. He muttered something and started to shake his head.

Joe moved up a couple of inches, watching the old man. "Don't stop now, Marty. What happened?"

Marty looked up. He fixed his gaze on a spot out at sea. "Out there. He asked if he could come out on the boat with me early one morning. He had a day off school. I told his mother I'd look after him. Everything was going well. We were about three miles offshore. The water was getting very choppy. He was complaining about feeling unwell. I told him to stand up at the front of the boat. Keep your eyes focused on the horizon, I told him. It'll settle your head. He was away standing up at the front. He thought he knew everything. He knew *nothing* about the sea. I always told him we had to show respect for the sea. It's far more powerful than we are, bigger and stronger. It can decide whether to let us live, or …"

Marty didn't finish what he was saying. He just brought his hands up to his face.

"What happened?" Joe asked, in a well-mannered way.

"Just as we banked over a sharp crest, a gust of wind blew him hard. He tripped on some fishing net on the bottom of the boat. He lost his balance and went over the side, right over the bow of the boat. I was out of the wheelhouse in a couple of seconds. I roared to the lads to throw the engines into reverse. It was only when I looked over the side that I realised how rough the sea was. Force four, maybe five. I jumped in close on the spot I reckoned he'd fallen in. I couldn't see him for ages. The water was crippling cold. I couldn't swim against the current. All the time I felt myself being sucked under. Then I saw him. He was down about fifteen feet. I took a deep breath and dived, hoping and praying I might reach him before my lungs exploded. It was inky black. I could barely see my hands."

Marty wiped the tears from his eyes.

"Did you reach him?" Joe asked.

"Yes, thank God. It seemed to take

ages. Seconds were like minutes. I felt like I'd been under the water for half an hour. All the time I was thinking of how much he was praying that I'd seen him going over. I knew he would be trying to call my name. Once I actually shouted his name, losing all the air I'd been trying to hold on to. I felt like I was choking to death, all the air sucked out of me."

"Was he OK?"

"Yes. The three lads on the boat pulled him back in. One of them had jumped in after me. He was OK after a few minutes. He had just swallowed a lot of water." Marty cleared his throat. "It's strange. I can see how much he has changed as a result of what happened to him that morning. And it shouldn't have to take something as awful as that to make you realise that life is here to be shared."

"Do you still see your son?"

"Oh yes, I see him every day. He lives in a town a few miles up the road from here. He's married now with a couple of boys of his own. He's a lot different these days. He knows the pain of loss. He's had his own fair share of hardships that he's had to learn to deal with on his own. And you know, Joe, there's nothing like an emergency to make you realise who's important to you and, more importantly, who you love."

Marty left it at that.

CHAPTER EIGHT

The two men sat quietly for a few minutes. They watched the seagulls racing each other. The birds ducked and dived, following the white wash of the two blue trawlers as they headed for the safety of the small harbour. In the distance, four or five miles maybe, they saw the majestic sight of the huge car ferry sweeping off the horizon.

"There's your boat, Joe. The one that's going to take you home to Liz and your new life together," Marty said softly.

"Don't remind me, Marty, please.

I'd love to stay here a bit longer. It's so peaceful."

Marty smiled. "I'm glad to see you're changing, Joe. It's going to take a while to change into the man you'll enjoy being. But it will happen." Marty leaned across and patted Joe's shoulder. "Tell me, what was the first thing that struck you when you saw Liz for the first time."

"Her smile."

"Didn't take you long to think of that."

"I remember where I saw her for the first time."

"Where was that?"

"I was in the supermarket where she worked, buying a few messages. I had my own place. My flatmate usually did all the shopping. He was away for a fortnight. So I had to get the groceries and all that kind of stuff. I hadn't a clue where everything was. She was stacking shelves. I was looking for a men's deodorant called Action. So when I said to her, 'Excuse me, I'm looking for Action,' she cracked up laughing. So did I."

Marty laughed heartily. "That's a good line. Very funny. I must remember that one."

"She told me it was the worst chat-up line she had ever heard. Anyway we chatted for a couple of minutes and I asked her out for a drink."

"That's a great story, Joe. How long ago was that?"

"Nine months ago."

Marty looked surprised. "You don't hang about, do you? Why did you both decide to get married so quickly?"

"It's a long story. My parents nearly freaked when they heard I was going out with a checkout assistant. My father's a doctor. My mother is a dentist. I'm their only child."

"I presume they wanted you to marry well."

Joe nodded. "They wanted me to study medicine. I rebelled and got a job delivering cars. I'd collect the cars from Birmingham and drive them back to Dublin, straight to their new owners' doorsteps. Eventually I saw how much profit my boss was making. I decided after a year or so to set up a dealership of my own."

"Good man. So you work long hours."

"Crazy hours. But I only intend doing it until –"

"I know – until you're thirty-five and living in Marbella on your luxury yacht," Marty cut in. "But why marry so quickly? What's the rush?"

"It was my way of getting up my

parents' noses. I really wanted to stick it to them. They hated Liz from the first day they met her. And I suppose I hated them for hating her. They hated her even before they met her. I remember my mother telling me that a woman with a Dublin accent had phoned for me. That's what my mother is like. She doesn't mind rooting around mouths belonging to people with Dublin accents. She'll happily take fifty quid out of their pockets, even though half of them can't afford it. But talk to them? Not on your life! She hates talking to anybody who doesn't have, as she puts it, a certain level of class. What a load of shite!"

Marty grinned. "You're not as bad as I first thought you were, Joe."

"What do you mean by that?"

"Well, you've got a heart. All I have to do now is find it. Do you love Liz?"

Joe pondered the question. "I don't know, Marty. I often ask myself that question. And when I do I try to avoid answering it. Because I don't think I do." Joe stared at Marty. "I never thought I'd say that to anybody. I used to think all blokes just got married and that was it. You stick a ring on her finger and you pick up where you left off before you said 'I do'. But I'm beginning to realise that it's not like that. I'm starting to think that this could change my whole life. Problem is, I like my life the way it is now. I don't want someone else tampering with the way I like to do things. I don't really know anybody close to me who is married. I don't call what my parents have a marriage. That's just some sort of sham they both seem happy to keep up. It's like they're the inventors and I'm their experiment.

"I still go over to them for Sunday dinner. They sit at each end of the table and I sit in the middle, and they prod me with their questions and probe me with their points of view. They never talk to each other, just criticise, or correct. Listening to the two of them is like reading a medical magazine. They're so full of their own bullshit, heaping it onto each other. I've never heard them laughing. I've never heard them saying to each other, 'Fancy going to the pub tonight?' like some of my mates' parents.

"They forced me to take piano lessons when I was two and a half. I gave them up when I was five. They insisted I learn the violin. I hated it. I threw in the towel when I failed my Grade One exams. I threw my violin into the back of the bin lorry one morning. They wouldn't hear of me playing football. Jesus, I hated them from the moment I could talk. I begged them to take me to the zoo. They asked a neighbour to take me. I pleaded with them to let me join the Boy Scouts. They said it was too rough; I might injure myself. I remember the day I threw myself out my friend's tree house that his father had built. I was chuffed waiting for my mother to open the hall door because I was covered in blood, just to see the look of horror on her face."

CHAPTER NINE

Joe stopped talking. "What time is it?"

Marty checked the battered old watch clinging to his wrist with a piece of blue ribbon. "It's twenty to eleven. Why?"

"Because I have to try and catch that boat back to Dublin. I'm not sure how I'm going to do it. But I'll try."

"Why do you want to go back if you don't love her?"

"What's the point of staying here?"

"Well, you seem to like it here. Am I right?"

"I feel good sitting here right now. I

didn't an hour ago. But I don't think that feeling will last much longer."

"Why do you enjoy sitting here?"

Joe thought about the question. "You're good company, some of the time."

"And the rest of the time?"

"You annoy me because you're right."

"You don't have to do anything you don't want to do, Joe. You know that, don't you?"

"Yes. But sometimes I'm afraid to do the things I'd really love to do."

"Why?"

"Because I'm afraid of ending up on my own for the rest of my life. I don't want to be lonely."

"You can be married with children, Joe, and still be the loneliest man in the world."

"So how can I avoid being lonely?"

"That's entirely up to you, Joe. It's all about realising that other people in your life are entitled to be treated the way you'd want them to treat you. Always do that and you'll never be lonely."

"I can't walk around dressed as Superman for the rest of my life. I have a business back in Dublin that needs me. And I have friends back there."

"Are they the same friends who poured you onto the car ferry last night?"

"I suppose so."

Marty hooted. "They don't sound like decent friends to me."

"They're OK. They just got carried away, I suppose. We all had too much to drink."

"But they all seem to have got home safely. Yet you're here on the other side of the Irish Sea." Marty scanned the cliff-top and the small park around them. "I don't see them coming looking for you to make sure you didn't fall overboard last night, or that you didn't die of the cold sleeping on this park bench in the early hours of the morning." Marty observed Joe for a moment. "Do you trust these so-called friends?"

"Not really," replied Joe.

"Well then, why do you hang around with them?"

Joe thought about the question. "I've never really given it much thought, I suppose."

"Do you ever feel lonely, Joe?"

"Do you?"

Marty shrugged. "Not really. I've had a good life. I have a few good friends. It's taken me a long time to find them. But at least now I know they'll be my friends forever, and I'll be theirs. It takes a heck of a long time to find a good friend. Would you agree?"

"Yeah."

"And another thing, get to like your own company. Don't be afraid of being on your own. Sometimes there's nothing I like better than talking to myself."

Joe nodded. "Yeah, you're right."

"Why do you hate your parents so much, Joe?"

"Because they never loved me."

"Did they tell you that?"

"No. But they never told me they loved me either."

"Have you ever tried to tell them that you love them?"

"Jesus, *no*! They'd collapse with the fright. I don't think the word 'love' exists in their dictionary."

"But surely they had to make love for you to be conceived?"

"Wrong. They had sex – a mechanical procedure whereby they followed a number of biological instructions and then they returned to their separate bedrooms."

Marty looked sad. "I can see where you took a wrong turn, Joe. And it wasn't your fault. Your parents really did bugger things up for you."

Joe looked shocked. "*Marty!*" he shouted. "Bad language doesn't suit you."

Marty laughed. "If you can use it, so can I."

By now, the two men were sitting close to each other.

CHAPTER TEN

An elderly woman shuffled past the park bench just as the old church clock was ringing eleven bells. She pushed an old supermarket trolley with a dog perched on the front end. She ignored the two men on the park bench. She muttered to herself and shook her head.

"God bless that poor woman," Marty said.

"Do you know her?" Joe asked.

"Know her very, very well. She's one of the kindest, sweetest people it's ever been my pleasure to know. I came from the street where she lives."

"Why didn't she look at us? She was only a couple of feet away when she passed us."

Marty watched her as she eased her trolley down the steep hill to the left of the small park. "She lost her husband a few years ago. Actually this day four years back, if I remember rightly. She never got over it. They were the closest couple I knew, always together. You couldn't get a breath of air between the two of them, they were so close," Marty said softly as she drifted out of view. "All the neighbours were very good. They tried and tried to help her get back to some sort of normal life. But she just turned inwards … kept to herself. Eventually she didn't bother going to church. She goes to the little shop at the bottom of the hill bright and early every morning before the town gets busy. Then she goes home again with her little dog. And that's it for another day." Marty looked back at Joe. "Medicine can cure all sorts of ailments these days, Joe – cancer, TB, smallpox, even brain tumours. But the most eminent men in the medical world can't find a cure for a broken heart." Marty sighed and deeply inhaled the bracing sea air. "And do you know why that is?"

Joe listened carefully. "Why?"

"Because buried deep in your heart is your soul. Your soul is the life-force of your body. It's what we get when we're conceived into this world, Joe. And it's what we hand back when God decides that it's time for us to go. But something strange happens to our souls when we meet the person we're destined to spend the rest of our lives with. Our feelings for that person are so intense that our souls unite. They can only survive after that with each other. They can't thrive alone. So when that someone you love with your heart and soul dies on you, Joe, often your soul dies with them. That's what's known as dying of a broken heart."

"But she's not dead."

"Look at her. She's barely hanging on. I wouldn't say it'd be too long before they're reunited. Would you?"

"I don't know."

"How do you think Liz would feel this morning if she were to get a phone call to say you'd been killed?"

"Jesus, Marty, I don't know! I don't normally spend my time thinking about morbid things like dying."

"We all die, Joe. It's no great shakes. It's just moving on to the next stage. Do you think she'd be upset?"

Joe thought uncomfortably. "Suppose she would be. She's planning on marrying me today. I guess she would."

"Now turn the tables. Would you cry if something terrible happened to Liz?"

"Of *course* I would. What sort of a question is that?"

"You told me just half an hour ago that you'd love to hear that she'd been killed."

Joe shivered and shook. "I didn't really mean what I said."

"It's getting a bit chilly up here. The wind is changing. I hope that ferry makes it into port before the wind shifts to an easterly direction," Marty said.

"Why's that?" asked Joe.

"Because if it starts blowing hard from the east, the ferry won't be able to sail."

"For how long?"

"For as long as it takes to change again." Marty looked at Joe with that wry, knowing smile. "You're not getting nervous, are you?"

"No I'm *not*!" Joe said adamantly.

"Nothing wrong with getting nervous on the day of your wedding, Joe. I'm sure Liz is feeling a few pangs of the old nerves right now. What do you think she's doing now?"

"Getting her hair done."

"How do you know that?"

"She told me she had an appointment at eleven in the hairdressers."

"Well done, you remembered that."

"It'd be difficult not to. She's been talking non-stop about today for the past three months."

"And what did the doctor and the dentist have to say when you told them you were marrying Liz?"

"My father freaked. He told me I

needed to have my head examined. Then he poured a large brandy for himself and one for my mother …"

"And your mother knocked your teeth out!" Marty almost fell off the bench he laughed so hard.

Joe started to laugh. "It's not funny."

"Of course it's funny, Joe. You're laughing, for God's sake. Enjoy it. It's meant to be the biggest day of your life." Marty became serious. "You told me earlier you didn't think you loved her. Why did you say that?"

Joe watched the ferry as it gave a long blow on its horn. "What does that mean?"

"It means he's ten minutes from docking. You didn't answer my question. Why did you say you didn't love her?"

"Because I'm afraid to give."

"Give *what*?"

"Commitment."

"Why?"

"Because I know once I give it I can't take it back without hurting her."

"You mean without breaking her heart?"

Joe nodded. "Yes."

"I think you've already given her a commitment. I also think you were happy to give her that commitment. Am I right?"

"Yes, I suppose I was. Do you know my parents threatened not to come to the wedding today?"

"You should have told them not to bother. They don't own you, Joe. They never owned you. From the moment you were born your life was mapped out. They have no say over what you think or do. Do you understand? You're probably thinking now that maybe they were right. Maybe Liz is not suitable for you, isn't that what you're thinking?"

"Yes."

"But you're only thinking that because you've been listening to what they've been telling you over and over for the last six months. You have to start listening to your heart, Joe. Because at some stage in life, that's the part of us we give away to someone else. We have to listen to what our heart is telling us. Not our parents, or our parents' views on life, but our *heart!*" Marty thumped his chest hard. "Right in there. Let that do the thinking for a little while and you'll be OK. What's the point in living in Marbella when you're thirty-five? All alone on the yacht that's going nowhere. Surrounded by people who your parents would love you to know, people you can't relate to. This is where you belong, Joe, sitting here having a heart-to-heart on a little park bench. Look around you, man. This is all here for you. And it's all *free*! It doesn't cost either of us a single penny. And all you have to do is sit back and enjoy it. I wouldn't ever swap this beautiful little pissed-on rusty park bench for a Marbella yacht. I don't know about you but this is home to me. This is where I lay my hat."

Joe smiled.

CHAPTER ELEVEN

"I'm going to have to say goodbye in a few minutes, Joe," Marty said. "That big mother of a boat's not going to hang around waiting, not even for Superman!"

Joe laughed. He felt sad at the notion of letting go of their time together. It had become something quite special. Very different to anything he had ever known. "Before you go, Marty." Joe waited for a moment before continuing. "Who are you?"

"Who do you think I am?" Marty asked.

"I don't know. I've never met

anyone like you in my life. You talk a lot of sense compared to the people I hang around with. They talk rubbish. They're full of their own self-importance."

"Like you were an hour ago, Joe. And you know that's all it takes to lose sight of who you are. I always keep back fifteen minutes for myself every day, just to sit on this little park bench. I try to remember certain things while I'm sitting here looking out at that beautiful sea. I remember that, like most things in life, that sea is so much bigger than me. I'm only a tiny pinhead in the scheme of things. But in another way this is all put here for me to enjoy and to learn from. What do you learn from selling cars?"

"Not a lot."

"Your heart's not in it, is it?"

"No."

"That's because your heart is trying

to tell you that there's so much more out there it wants you to see and feel. You don't have to travel to Marbella to feel your heart beating wildly. Let your heart take the lead, Joe, and see where it takes you. I bet you'll be amazed by what happens." Marty leaned across the bench and pinched Joe's cheek. "Where are you going to take her on your honeymoon?" he asked.

"Marbella," Joe replied cheekily.

They both roared laughing.

"I think your parents have raised a good man."

"I think I'm a fool and I've a lot to learn."

"Hey, don't knock the learning. I'm eighty-three and I've got a lot to learn yet. You know what you should do when you're giving your little speech this afternoon? You should start off by saying, 'Ladies and gentlemen, I have keep in touch with you?" Joe asked Marty.

"For what?" Marty asked.

"I'd just like to ring you the odd time," Joe said.

"No you wouldn't," Marty said bashfully.

"I would."

"I'm not connected," Marty replied.

"Well, is there an address I can write to you at?"

Marty laughed. "Sure you don't even know me, kid. What would you want to say to me in a letter?"

Joe couldn't find an answer to the question. "What am I going to tell them at the ferry?"

"Nothing." Marty rooted in his inside ket. "Here, I found this last night. Is urs?" He gave the coupon to Joe. was speechless. It was his return 'Where did you find it?"

just one thing to say to my parents today. Mom and Dad, I've never said this to either of you before, and I want to say it right now: I love you both.' I think they'd really appreciate that, Joe."

Joe laughed off the notion. "You must be joking. They'd fall off their chairs with embarrassment."

"I bet they wouldn't, Joe. And I'll tell you something else. I reckon they'll both say it back to you at some stage this evening. We can have a little bet if you don't believe me."

"Forget it."

"I can't, Joe. I want you to know a couple of things before you leave here this morning and return to Dublin. Your parents might seem a bit odd to you. They might not have done everything your mates' parents did for them. But in their own way, they would die for you. Here's another thing. Liz loves you. I know that."

"How do you know that?"

"I know by the way you talk about her. You're in awe of her. She scares you because she loves you so much. She's gotten the hang of this 'heart' business. She knows where she wants to put her heart. And believe it or not, it's in your court right now, and will be forever. All you've got to do is let your heart go. Believe me, it feels like magic when you do it." Marty stood up. "Listen to Liz. She'll teach you all about life. Now go down there and catch that boat."

CHAPTER TWELVE

The old woman watched the gate of the small park that led to the edge of the cliffs overlooking the choppy The sun was high in the sky raised her hand to shield her the glare. She studied the as he rambled down pebbled path, wearing and red tights. She him on television mind had st couldn't pl "Hav

"Blowing across the park when I arrived for my walk this morning. I chased it to the edge of the cliff. Just grabbed it in time." He searched his other pocket. "Here, I don't have much money. Take this tenner. You might need it." He handed the money to Joe.

"I can't take that."

"Go on, buy yourself a coffee and some breakfast. You need it more than I do. Anyway I've got a few bob locked up at home. Don't worry about me. Just get yourself sorted out. I reckon if the ferry leaves on time, you should be in Dublin shortly before two. That gives you an hour to get yourself looking respectable. Don't keep her waiting."

The two men turned to each other. First they shook hands warmly. Then they hugged.

Marty stepped back and rubbed his

nose. "I've enjoyed meeting you, Joe. Have a good life and tell that woman of yours at least once a day that you love her. OK?"

Joe nodded. "I will. I hope to see you again, Marty."

"Don't worry. I'm here if you need me." Marty pointed over his shoulder to the park bench on the hilltop.

Joe waved to Marty and started his long walk to the ferry. He slowed down and looked back, just where the pebbled path met the main road to the port.

Marty was gone.

CHAPTER THIRTEEN

The port of Holyhead was teeming with passengers coming off the Dublin ferry on one side, and the passengers waiting to board, in an orderly queue, standing patiently on the other. Three girls started to wolf whistle when they saw Joe.

"Hey Superman," one of them shouted, "can you make this queue move any quicker?"

The long line of people laughed and applauded.

Once the queue started to move, it didn't take long for Joe to get to the point of presenting his ticket. The port police gave him a few strange looks.

"Where are you travelling to, Superman?"

"Dublin. I'm getting married this afternoon," Joe answered politely.

"To who? Lois Lane?" one of the guards joked. It was their turn to laugh.

Just as Joe was about to walk through the departure doors, he stepped back. "Excuse me," he said to one of the guards who had just checked his ticket.

"Yes, sir."

"Are you from Holyhead?" Joe asked.

"I am."

"Do you know an elderly man called Marty? Sits up on the park bench every morning close to the cliffs?"

The guard seemed uncomfortable. He looked to the other guards, then back to Joe. "Yes, I know him very well. Why do you ask?"

"I've just spent the most fascinating hour of my life in his company. Next time you see him, tell him that he's one of the finest men I've ever met."

"And your name is …?"

"Joe – Joe Mooney."

"It's very kind of you to say those things about my father, Joe. But I think you must be mixing him up with someone else. Marty died four years ago. Actually today is the fourth anniversary of his death." The guard was getting quite choked up. "He drowned in a boating accident."

Joe froze. "He dived in to save you?"

The guard nodded. "My father was one in a million, a very special man. He always thought with his heart, he used to tell me. Unfortunately, I only found out what he meant by that after he had gone. They all say the same thing about Marty: he had a big heart and time for everybody. Just before you go, do you mind me asking how you knew about my father saving me?"

Joe thought for a moment. He was about to tell him. He decided not to. "I read it somewhere."

CHAPTER FOURTEEN

The flowers on the altar reminded Joe of the small park he had spent the morning in, overlooking the sea. Dermot, his best man, stood to his right. Liz's mother sat across the aisle to his left. The organ music started.

"Why are you out of breath?" Dermot asked again, "Are you going to tell me what happened to you?"

Joe shook his head. "I just bumped into someone I knew. He gave me a few quid. I got back on the boat and here I am. OK?" Joe looked around to check the clock at the back of the church. He gasped. His first sighting of the woman he was about to marry.

He thought of the things he had said earlier in the day. He couldn't figure out why he had said them. His heart pounded as she linked his arm.

"Look after her," her father said.

Joe grinned.

For a moment it was the sound of Marty's voice.

OPEN DOOR SERIES
SERIES ONE

Sad Song by Vincent Banville
In High Germany by Dermot Bolger
Not Just for Christmas by Roddy Doyle
Maggie's Story by Sheila O'Flanagan
Jesus and Billy Are Off to Barcelona
by Deirdre Purcell
Ripples by Patricia Scanlan

SERIES TWO

No Dress Rehearsal by Marian Keyes
Joe's Wedding by Gareth O'Callaghan
It All Adds Up by Margaret Neylon
Second Chance by Patricia Scanlan
Pipe Dreams by Anne Schulman
Old Money, New Money by Peter Sheridan

just one thing to say to my parents today. Mom and Dad, I've never said this to either of you before, and I want to say it right now: I love you both.' I think they'd really appreciate that, Joe."

Joe laughed off the notion. "You must be joking. They'd fall off their chairs with embarrassment."

"I bet they wouldn't, Joe. And I'll tell you something else. I reckon they'll both say it back to you at some stage this evening. We can have a little bet if you don't believe me."

"Forget it."

"I can't, Joe. I want you to know a couple of things before you leave here this morning and return to Dublin. Your parents might seem a bit odd to you. They might not have done everything your mates' parents did for them. But in their own way, they would die for you. Here's another thing. Liz loves you. I know that."

"How do you know that?"

"I know by the way you talk about her. You're in awe of her. She scares you because she loves you so much. She's gotten the hang of this 'heart' business. She knows where she wants to put her heart. And believe it or not, it's in your court right now, and will be forever. All you've got to do is let your heart go. Believe me, it feels like magic when you do it." Marty stood up. "Listen to Liz. She'll teach you all about life. Now go down there and catch that boat."

CHAPTER TWELVE

The old woman watched the gate of the small park that led to the edge of the cliffs overlooking the choppy sea. The sun was high in the sky as she raised her hand to shield her eyes from the glare. She studied the young man as he rambled down the narrow, pebbled path, wearing a yellow cape and red tights. She remembered seeing him on television many years ago. Her mind had started to wander and she couldn't place his name.

"Have you a number I can ring to

keep in touch with you?" Joe asked Marty.

"For what?" Marty asked.

"I'd just like to ring you the odd time," Joe said.

"No you wouldn't," Marty said bashfully.

"I would."

"I'm not connected," Marty replied.

"Well, is there an address I can write to you at?"

Marty laughed. "Sure you don't even know me, kid. What would you want to say to me in a letter?"

Joe couldn't find an answer to the question. "What am I going to tell them at the ferry?"

"Nothing." Marty rooted in his inside pocket. "Here, I found this last night. Is it yours?" He gave the coupon to Joe.

Joe was speechless. It was his return ticket. "Where did you find it?"